Skippyjon Jones
COSTUME CRAZEE
STICKER STORIES

Based on the *Skippyjon Jones* series
created by Judy Schachner

Grosset & Dunlap

978-0-448-45168-8   10 9 8 7 6 5 4

Skippyjon Jones can't wait for Halloween!
He's decorated his room, but he still
doesn't know what to wear.

"You should be a *pirata*!" Don Diego says. Skippyjon thinks about it, but a *pirata* doesn't seem right.

Poquito Tito says, "Be a mummito, Skippito."
Skippyjon thinks about all the *chicharos* he could
hold in his wraps, but a mummito is wrong, too.

Los Chimichangos shout out suggestions . . . "How about a ghost or a zombito . . . Dress yourself as El Bumblebeeto . . . Think of all the candy you'll get to eat-o!" But Skippyjon doesn't like these ideas, either.

"What should I be for Halloween?" Skippyjon asks his sisters.
"Dress as a bunny!" cries Jilly Boo, who likes anything cute.
"A bunny?" says Skippyjon. "No way, José!"

10

"I have an idea, Mr. Silly Britches," Mama Junebug Jones says. "Why don't you dress as a jack-o'-lantern?" Hmmm . . .

Skippyjon has a lot of thinking to do, so he goes for a bounce on his big-boy bed. He bounces once, he bounces twice, and the third time he bounces he says:

"Oh, I'm Skippyjon Jones
And I bounce here and there,
But I just can't decide
What costume to wear."

14

Suddenly, Skippyjon has an idea. "Holy jalapeño," he cries. "I know just what to be . . ."

"I'll dress up as a Siamese cat!"
Skippyjon puts on his costume
and out he goes with his friends.
"Trick or treat!"

Use these stickers
on pages 2-3

Use these stickers
on pages 4-5

Use these stickers
on pages 6-7

Use these stickers
on pages 8-9

Use these stickers
on pages 10-11

Use these stickers
on pages 12-13

Use these stickers
on pages 14-15

Use these stickers
on page 16